Lisa
Comes to the Rescue

Zuza Vrbova

Illustrated by Tom Morgan-Jones

CHRYSALIS CHILDREN'S BOOKS

Lisa loved vehicles. She liked cars. She liked tractors.
She liked helicopters, aeroplanes, scooters, motorbikes,
speedboats and trains – especially steam trains. In fact,
Lisa liked anything that had wheels, moved and went fast!

MY MOTOR MAGAZINE

4

She knew everything that there was to know about vehicles
– she was always reading My Motor Magazine. And if Lisa
wasn't reading about vehicles, she was playing with them.

Lisa had her own fleet of vehicles. Her favourites were Scottie Scooter, Tracy Tractor, Henry Helicopter and Fiona Fire Engine.

"Scottie, you are small and speedy. Overtake Tracy and squeeze into that narrow parking space!" Lisa commanded as she pushed Scottie along her bedroom floor.

Then she turned to her tractor and said,

"Tracy, you've worked so hard, ploughing the fields all day long! You can leave the farm now and play with your friends Henry and Fiona!"

7

Lisa's family liked to go for picnics in the countryside. The best bit for Lisa was the journey.

"Will you play Spot The Car with me?" she always asked her older brother, Luke.

"Oh, all right," replied Luke, yawning.

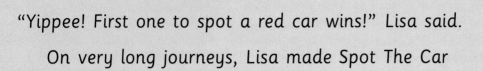

"Yippee! First one to spot a red car wins!" Lisa said.

On very long journeys, Lisa made Spot The Car a bit harder.

"First one to spot a classic car!"

Or "First one to spot an Italian motorbike!"

One day, Lisa was walking to school with Peter
as usual. Suddenly, a flash of colour and
a burst of noise whizzed past them.

"Hey! Did you see that?" Lisa shouted.

"That was a Red Rocket Sport! There are only eight
in the whole country! It's a limited-edition motorbike!"

Peter sighed. This happened every day.

Cars and motorbikes all looked the same to him.

He began to walk faster. Lisa was left behind –
she was still staring after the Red Rocket Sport.

The first lesson was geography. Miss Roo was spinning a big globe in front of the class. "This is our world," she explained.

Immediately, Lisa piped up,
"The round-the-world record
on a motorbike is 19 days!"

Peter sighed and rolled his eyes.

"We're not talking about motorbikes
right now, Lisa," Miss Roo said gently.

Next it was art and design. Lauren was
making some bones out of clay.

"Can you help me make a dinosaur skeleton?"
she asked Lisa.

"No. I'm busy. I'm making some rotor blades for
my helicopter," Lisa replied without looking up.

14

"Your helicopter looks like an old dinosaur anyway!" interrupted Crispin with his usual charm.

Lisa was too busy to pay any attention to him.

Then Bertie said to Lisa, "I'm building a robot. Can you help me?"

"No. I'm making some gears now," she answered.

One day, Lisa was walking home from school.

She saw old Mr Price lying under a car, covered in oil.

"Wow! That's an original Series-1 Landie!"

Lisa said.

"Yup, you might be right," Mr Price mumbled.

"Do you want to borrow my spanner?"

Lisa asked, pulling it out of her bag.

(She never went anywhere without her spanner.)

"Well, yes, I suppose that would be useful,"
said Mr Price, taking the spanner.

"I've seen a picture of your car before,
but I've never seen a real one," Lisa chattered on.

Mr Price just grumbled and mumbled as usual.

17

The next day, at lunchtime,

Lisa went over to Lauren, Bertie and Roddy.

"Do you want to help me polish my car?"
she asked them.

"No, of course we don't!" Roddy said.
"We've got better things to do, Lisa the Loser!"
And he stomped off.

"You're not interested in my dinosaur bones,"
said Lauren quietly.

"Or my robot," said Bertie. "So why should
we be interested in your car?"

They went to play on the climbing frame.

Suddenly, Lisa didn't feel like polishing her car either.
She sat under the oak tree and read My Motor Magazine.

After lunch, Miss Roo made an announcement,
"Next week we are going on a school trip –
to the dinosaur museum!"

　　Everyone cheered. Everyone, that is, except Lisa.
She groaned. Loudly.

　　"Can't we go to the transport museum instead?"
she asked. "I want to see a biplane and a steam train and..."

20

"...and a lawn mower?" interrupted Crispin.

"Because they are REALLY interesting,"

he said sarcastically.

Everyone laughed.

"Lisa is right," said Miss Roo.

"The transport museum is full of interesting things.

Perhaps we can go there another time."

The next week, the whole class got on the bus
to go to the dinosaur museum.

Tabby was conducting a loud sing-song.

"The wheels on the bus go round
and round..." everyone sang together.

"Come on, Lisa, join in!"
shouted Tabby.

But Lisa wasn't listening to Tabby.
She was listening to the bus. It was
making some very strange noises.
And she could see dark smoke
coming out of the engine.

The bus began to climb up
a steep hill, very, very slowly.

When the bus was almost at the top of the hill,
it began to shudder and shake. The bus driver
parked the bus by the side of the road and jumped out.

"I'm not sure what the problem is," he said,
lifting the bonnet and scratching his head.

Lisa jumped out of the bus and looked at the engine too.

"I think it's a problem with the carburettor,"
she said. "Let's take it out and give it a clean."

25

"But I don't have any tools," said the bus driver.

"No worries!" said Lisa, pulling her spanner
out of her bag. She carefully unbolted the big,
round carburettor.

"You're right, it is very dirty," said the bus driver.

Lisa and the driver cleaned the carburettor
with a rag and, using Lisa's spanner, gently put it
back in the engine. The whole class was watching.

Everyone got back on the bus and the driver turned the key.

The bus roared back to life with a healthy chugging noise.

"That sounds better!" said Lisa. "We can get going now."

"Hurray for Lisa!" the class shouted.

For the rest of the journey, everyone wanted to have a look at Lisa's spanner. She handed it around proudly.

When they got to the museum, Lauren pointed at the huge

skeleton in the hall. "That's a diplodocus," she said.

"It looks so fierce!" said Lisa, looking at its teeth.

"It was actually quite gentle," said Lauren wisely.

"And it ate only plants!"

Lisa couldn't take her eyes
off the skeleton.

It's as complicated as an engine, she thought.

"Next time you need help putting together
your clay bones, let me know!" she said to Lauren smiling.

Top of the Class

Collect them all!

Ellie Takes a Chance
Zuza Vrbova
Illustrated by Tom Morgan-Jones
1-84458-483-6

Zoë Wins the Race
Zuza Vrbova
Illustrated by Tom Morgan-Jones
1-84458-407-0

Piers Finds his Voice
Zuza Vrbova
Illustrated by Tom Morgan-Jones
1-84458-406-2

George Makes Friends
Zuza Vrbova
Illustrated by Tom Morgan-Jones
1-84458-482-8

Lisa Comes to the Rescue
Zuza Vrbova
Illustrated by Tom Morgan-Jones
1-84458-578-6

Tabby Saves the Day
Zuza Vrbova
Illustrated by Tom Morgan-Jones
1-84458-481-X

Kit Paints the Sky
Zuza Vrbova
Illustrated by Tom Morgan-Jones
1-84458-404-6

Leo Takes to the Stage
Zuza Vrbova
Illustrated by Tom Morgan-Jones
1-84458-405-4

Roddy Learns a Lesson
Zuza Vrbova
Illustrated by Tom Morgan-Jones
1-84458-480-1

Fay Goes to the Dance
Zuza Vrbova
1-84458-579-4

Visit the Top of the Class website at
www.topoftheclassbooks.com